The Crane's Tale

The Crane's Tale

by Don Crane

The Pentland Press
Edinburgh – Cambridge – Durham – USA

First published in 1999 by
The Pentland Press Ltd
1 Hutton Close
South Church
Bishop Auckland
Durham

ISBN 1-85821-652-4

The Crane's Tale

Typeset in Goudy 10/12
by Carnegie Publishing, Carnegie House, Chatsworth Road, Lancaster
Printed and bound by Antony Rowe Ltd, Chippenham

To John

Contents

List of Illustrations

Foreword

I T SHOULD COME AS NO SURPRISE when a friend and business associate of twenty-two years discovers a new outlet for a talent-in-waiting. I met Don Crane in 1976 and was privileged to participate in a few winter activities similar to those described in this wonderful collection of short stories.

Don was a geophysicists' geophysicist and a seasoned campaigner in the business of oil and gas exploration in Western and Arctic Canada. The stories here ring true and must surely find a place in the documented literature that relates to the business of life; to life in Western Canada and to the experience of a career in the pioneering days of exploration in the Arctic.

This collection of short stories is a wonderful ensemble of human experience and the natural ability of the author to capture the right amount of detail to bring each story to life. The meticulous choice of word and phrase brings a special touch that keeps the reader engrossed till the last sentence of each adventure. The book will find a market with anyone who likes a good yarn or is curious about Canada's north country.

Dr A. Easton Wren
Calgary, Alberta, Canada
August 21, 1998

Preface

THE TALES SET DOWN in this volume reflect some memories of my early
years. At present I am savouring retirement near Calgary after enjoying
a career searching for petroleum in many untamed and fascinating places.
For the most part the stories deal with activities that were undertaken in
the harsh environment of Northern Canada. Some tales, however, deal with
experiences enjoyed in more pleasurable settings.

My life has been extremely interesting and I am very grateful to the
Almighty for having given me such great parents, a wonderful century in
which to live and for allowing me to find Vi, my loving wife of forty-five
years.

This compilation is dedicated to my best friend, John, who has kept my
mind attuned to things eternal.

Don Crane

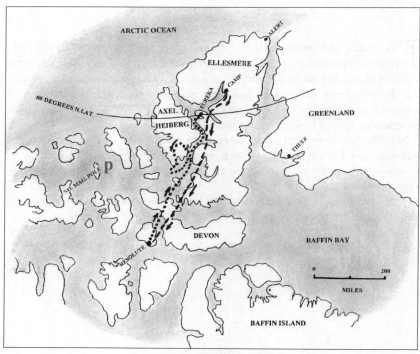

ARCTIC OCEAN

ALERT

ELLESMERE

EUREKA CAMP

80 DEGREES N.LAT.

AXEL HEIBERG

GREENLAND

THULE

NO. MAG. POLE

p

DEVON

BAFFIN BAY

RESOLUTE

0   200

MILES

BAFFIN ISLAND

Canada's High Arctic islands.

High Arctic Adventure

T HE STAGE WAS SET FOR DISASTER and little did I know that my name
was on the script. Gil, the pilot, and I had set out on a routine grocery
flight from our camp on northern Ellesmere Island in Canada's High Arctic.
On that day in July 1970 our destination was Resolute, five hundred miles
to the south.

Beautiful summer, perpetual sunlight, a carefree heart and a sturdy single
engine Beaver seemed like a great combination. After an uneventful flight
we arrived in Resolute and proceeded to greatly overload our willing little
plane with groceries, spare parts, mail and propane tanks. Having sacrificed
some fuel in order to lift the wheels off the ground we struggled into the
bright blue sky for our return trip to camp.

What a fantastic, contented feeling to fly along at 3,000 feet, skirting
Cornwallis and Devon islands with their ice-packed inlets and channels.
Now and then a few muskoxen would lumber around into protective rings.
A scrawny white wolf would lope along and the bouncy hares zipped away
at full tilt on their hind legs.

All seemed familiar and unforeboding until the true nature of the High
Arctic decided to assert itself and throw a few roadblocks at us – just for
fun! To us, however, the ominous black band of clouds directly on our path
was not funny at all.

Gil said, 'See if we have any decent maps to look at.'

His tone of voice had changed and I, becoming quite attentive, searched
for and found a small scale, partially shredded map of Axel Heiberg and
Ellesmere islands. I spotted our location and put my finger on 'here'. We
were past the point of return to Resolute and there were no landing sites
before the Eureka weather base. We would have to press on.

At this juncture the clouds decided to drop and suddenly we were in the
opaque mass. Gil spluttered, 'We will have to dive below this because I can't
see.'

Eureka Sound is a very long, rather narrow, sinuous stretch of water and
ice flanked by sheer cliffs of solid rock. Our intention was to follow this

The sturdy Beaver aircraft at the Tanquary Fiord Camp, fitted with both skis and wheels. In the background is a single-engined Otter.

feature to where it ended at Eureka. It was miles from our Tanquary Fiord camp but at least we could land and wait out the storm. Quickly descending to about 300 feet we saw open water and the massive cliffs but also noted they were being covered by the churning clouds. The sensation was that of being in a cloud-capped tunnel with walls of rock, water and ice.

My stalled heart began to beat again only to be interrupted by the ever lowering roof of clouds. In about a minute we were forced to fly at the dangerous level of 50 feet above the water with barely enough room to avoid the cliffs. After a quick glance at Gil I felt my seat being compressed by the rapid uplift of the plane as he poured on the power and we ascended, blindfolded, up into the clouds.

I saw the altimeter, our only useful instrument, spin to 5,000 feet. The earth's magnetic pole, somewhere to the southwest of us, kept our compass in a state of confusion and we had only our senses to determine or remember our direction. We climbed slowly to 10,000 feet at which time the engine coughed and appeared ready for a rest. Finally at 11,000 feet Gil yelled, 'We will stall if we try to climb higher.'

The clouds were still with us and as thick as pea soup. Gil reckoned we were heading north over southern Axel Heiberg but fleetingly added, 'I think.'

I pondered our plight. The plane was icing up and we were wandering on a seat-of-our-pants course over glaciers with no radio contact. I kept looking at the map and found to my alarm there was no elevation indicated for the mountains. They may have been just beside us or, what was even more frightful, just in front of us.

What to do—? Obviously we had to descend. Gil banked to the left and we drifted downward, straining our eyes to see that which we dared not see. After an eternity we broke out of the clouds to see water and ice floes 100 feet below. In five minutes a familiar spit of land showed our course to be wrong, going westward into oblivion.

We decided to try for Eureka Sound again and take our chances on traversing the 'tunnel', no matter how small. On a replotted course we skimmed over the ice and water and finally re-entered the cloud-covered channel with sharpened wits and the determination of the explorers of old.

We flew quietly northwards around the cliffs and promontories under the clouds which were being supported by our guardian angels between 100 and 300 feet.

The Beaver droned on at 90 mph, as did our hearts. Miraculously the tunnel remained open for 130 miles and our fuel held.

Finally we spotted Slidre Fiord, banked right, found Eureka and plopped down onto the most welcome runway in the whole wide world. Safe at last. Then we dove into a case of tomato juice and raised a thankful toast to the frazzled pair of adventurers who flew the milk run to Resolute.

Gil, the pilot, with a musk ox skull in front of his tent.

Two Fish Stories

THERE ONCE WAS A FAMILY WHO LOVED FISH. They enjoyed tropical varieties seen on their holidays in the Caribbean, but the true love of fish was in the eating. Good firm fish from the far northern lakes and streams were just heaven. A big jumbo whitefish, or perhaps a succulent Arctic char prepared in the optimal way set rumbles of joy in tummies. Better yet was a grayling just out of a fast stream.

There was a dark side to such fantasizing about such highly edible fish because the family had recently moved to the deep south . . . Calgary, and fish of this nature were rarely on their table. Father would sit thinking about the good old days spent in Canada's north and how the fish smelled in the pan and how the taste sent shivers up and down. Oh if only . . .

Well, as time passed he was called to business on the Beaufort Sea, in the winter of 1968. Not much chance of casting a line into a rushing stream or even trolling on the open water. Ice pervaded and the landscape was bleak. Fish were the last thing to think about.

The boss had said, 'We have to know if we can explore for oil on the ice pack.' They mobilized and went north.

A crew was hired to drill holes through the eight foot ice, and to lower and explode dynamite in the water below. It seemed a very stupid thing to do, as seen by the Eskimo guide, but it did have a purpose. Seismic recordings were taken in an effort to locate structures deep below the surface. The dynamite provided energy for sound waves to be generated and reflected. Dynamite! What a dastardly product. It did help in exploration but what about the fish! Ah, fish, what an interesting subject!

It seemed that some other group had thought of the possibility of fish kill and sure enough the Government men arrived. They were thought of as being important, at least by their companions, but really Father considered them a bloody nuisance. What could they possibly do that had any of the so called importance? Well, the conversation centred around environment, needless slaughter of wild life, revoking licences to drill, etc. The operation was shut down until these matters could be settled and that did seem important.

Two of the five
fish ready to
hop into the
sleeping bag.

It was decided that a survey of fish population would be undertaken immediately and if fish were found in abundance then, perhaps, the operation would be suspended. Eskimos were commissioned to set nets below the ice to ensnare whatever laid below.

A day went by. Nets were recovered and what a harvest. Father stood entranced. There was a quintet of the most interesting, long nosed, pure, big and obviously luscious and savory fish that ever lay on ice. The survey was now in deep trouble. Government stood around the quick-freezing specimens nodding heads and making momentous decisions.

Should the multi-thousand dollar survey be suspended, and if so, how could they face the ire of the big oil company and still report to their superiors? This became a sensitive, political predicament. It was five fish against progress. A huddle then formed, words were muted, workers stood like statues and Father salivated and hoped.

A junior autocrat was heard to whisper 'species', and 'only five'.

Hearing this, the dynamite shooter concluded, and murmured to his mates, 'These five fish are the last of their species!'

Hush! A decision had been made. The leading bureaucrat stated simply, 'Proceed with the operation.'

Father felt the flutter in his stomach. What would be the fate of the quints?

It was further stated by the potentates, 'These fish are not to be returned to the ocean depths nor taken to headquarters. They are to be left, as is, to the scavengers.'

Now all and sundry at the site lost interest in that subject and eagerly fell upon their dynamite. Boom, boom and the group hastened off to another part of the ice pack. Not Father however. He was busy frantically recalling the definition of 'scavenger' and joyfully concluded that he fitted the bill!

How was he to transport them home? Then he remembered his sleeping bag in the helicopter a mere quarter mile away. At a fast dog trot and with many huffs and puffs he set off, removed his sleeping bag and returned with the sturdy outer pull-string bag. Would you believe it? Five fish were the same size as a 5-star eiderdown sleeping bag. Draw-string in place, the scavenger puffed back to the 'copter.

Returning to Calgary the next week was a breeze. Frozen fish in the declared luggage earned a place in the sub-zero storage compartment. The next thing you knew his happy wife Vi was serving a steaming platter of a baked, luscious, delectable, Arctic fish, ' . . . the last of its species!'

On another northern jaunt Father found himself marking time in the Hay River settlement on the banks of Lake Athabasca. After a long session in the field doing survey work he was itching to get home. However plane connections in the old days were really not dependable and a long wait was announced. As usual the air was crisp and the mercury said minus 33 but his parka was thick and his boots cozy. He wandered along the main part of the small town, looking in the windows and chatting with everyone he met.

Finally he reached the town limits but noticed a small Indian village further on and kept strolling towards it. He was interested in the buildings with wood smoke drifting out of galvanised chimneys, various dog sleds, piles of cut poplar firewood and the irregular streets. At most homes a pack of curled-up husky dogs was silently sleeping. Not a person was in sight.

Father murmured to himself, 'I wish I could talk to some dog sled driver to find out the nature of those beasts.'

Just then he stopped short. Could that be a pile of fish stacked against that modest little house? Surely they couldn't be jumbo whitefish. (Jumbos were the elite of the whitefish clan and so much different from the smaller, tasteless variety found in more temperate climes, down south. They had a pronounced hump behind their head, flesh was firmer and the taste . . . wonderful.)

With this new interest he became quite bold. He strode up to the little door and knocked.

'Hello there,' he said to a very small, middle aged native who opened the door. Immediately he was invited in and asked to sit. The host was most friendly and the two began the slow process of talking. No questions, only circumlocutory hints as to each other's well being, the weather and other generalities.

Finally Father got nearer to the point of his interest and said, 'I noticed a great pile of whitefish against your house.'

'Yah,' replied the other, 'they are for my dogs. I catch them in the big lake and they freeze good.'

'Dogs indeed,' thought Father. 'What I wouldn't give for a bag full of dog food.' Further skirting of the subject took place until the visitor felt he would explode with expectation. He finally asked if he could buy some of the jumbos, for himself to eat.

'Sure, I have lots,' replied the native.

Now two problems arose: what would be the exorbitant price and how to transport them home? It was decided that Father would have to get a bag. Off he went to the town and bought two gunny sacks at the local hardware. He hired a taxi (no expense spared!) and returned to his new-found friend. After filling the large bags they sat down over price negotiations.

Father thought the 120 pounds would be a bit over his budget but finally heard his host say, 'How about twelve dollars?' Well, that was so low that he countered with, 'I will up that to fifteen dollars if you help me into the taxi.' Good . . . deal finished.

Racing back to the airport Father caught the plane just in time. Now you can imagine the scene around the supper table, Vi and girls beaming and Don sitting back with such a smug, satisfied smile . . . and full tummies all around. The frozen beauties lasted all winter.

— 3 —

A Moosehide Christmas

CHRISTMAS WAS JUST TWO WEEKS AWAY and my wife and three little girls were a thousand miles south while I was on a job in Canada's far north. I planned to return the day before the BIG day to be with them. Vi had bought the Christmas presents but still wanted something else for the little ones. What to get? Birch bark, raven feathers and scrub brush seemed to be the only things available and these were not too exciting.

The next day, trudging through the low forest, I saw smoke and a small Native Indian shack. All were friends in the North so I knocked on the door and was invited in for tea.

An ancient grandmother sat on the floor making a pair of moosehide mitts. The moosehide had been tanned over dense smoke from damp willow and spruce branches. It sent forth a strong, characteristic, smoky aroma that filled the whole house. I sat with her and after a long time asked if she made other things. 'Yes,' she replied, 'I make good mukluks.' The light went on in my brain, here was the answer.

She was happy to hear of my three girls, aged three, six and eight. Yes, she could make three pairs in three days if she had enough moosehide, coloured thread and stroud (the thick felt-like, white wool). Scrounging about she came up with this raw material and all was well – except for the sizes.

In Cree she yelled, 'Astum', and in came seven grandchildren of many sizes. She said, 'Point out the ones,' so I selected three about the right height and foot size.

The next week I returned with abundant oranges, paid the dear old Nookum and left for home. You can imagine the happiness, excitement and love that flowed around our Christmas tree as the rich smelling, fresh moosehide mukluks were unwrapped.

Now, thirty-five years later, at Christmas, grandchildren still parade around in well worn, ragged but precious mukluks.

4

A Story from Far Away

This factual/fictionalized account was written for my grand-daughter, Robena Turner, age 6, to make her acquainted with her Great Grandfather Charlie Gratama (1905–1984).

ONCE UPON A TIME IN A KINGDOM CALLED HOLLAND a happy event took place. But before hearing this you must know that Holland is in Europe, close to Germany and across the sea from England. Holland is a flat country and has a LOT of water. There are rivers and canals but also the ocean laps its shores. There are big cities like Amsterdam and Rotterdam but this story takes place in a little village called Pingjum (pronounced Ping-um).

Well, as I said there was a happy event in Pingjum one day in 1875, more than a hundred years ago. Everyone was happy because a little boy was born into the family of Tjepke (Chep-ka) and Eelke (El-key) Gratama. His name was Rients (Ree-ents) and was he ever cute. He had very blue eyes and very blond hair and good strong hands. Eelke said he looked like his dad.

Little Rients grew quickly and when he was three another happy family just down the street had a baby girl. She was called Wiepkje (Veep-key) Fopma and guess what! She had blue eyes and very blond hair too. Little Rients ran down the cobblestone street and peeked in the Fopmas' window and saw the beautiful baby. He told his dog, Woopsy, that he was going to marry that girl someday but not to tell anyone just yet.

Both these two little Fries children grew and grew. They went to school but also had to work for their parents. Rients' dad, Tjepke was a farmer who grew flax and Wiepkje's dad grew tulips. One day Rients' dad said, 'My son, you will not go to school this week because we must cut the flax and tramp the stems down into the water in the canal.'

Rients said, 'Why bury the good stems? They may get all rotten.'

'Ah, my big boy, that is how to make linen, which your mum needs to make our clothes.'

Houses in Pingjum, Netherlands, with the kirk in the background.

Just then Wiepkje came up, quite excited, and said she had to help her Mum pick tulips for selling and she would not see Rients for a whole week. After that she also had to help dig potatoes, sob, sob.

One sunny day Wiepkje and Rients walked down to see the big ocean where the waves splashed against the shore. Rients wondered what was under the water and Wiepkje said that her uncle told her it had been good farm land but now was no good anymore since the big storm.

'Oh, tell me what happened,' said Rients.

'Well,' said Wiepkje. 'My uncle Pieter said that six hundred years ago all this was good farm land and all the great Zuyder Zee was not even here then. Our land, Holland, was much bigger and the ocean was far to the north. Then in 1286 there was a terribly big storm that lasted for many days and the wind blew and the ocean waves got bigger and bigger. Finally the shore and sand and trees were washed away and the ocean rushed onto the farm land. Many people were drowned and all the cows and chickens were washed away. When it was over the people that were left looked out and all they saw was water. They were very unhappy and called the water the "Zuyder Zee". Since then our country was much smaller.'

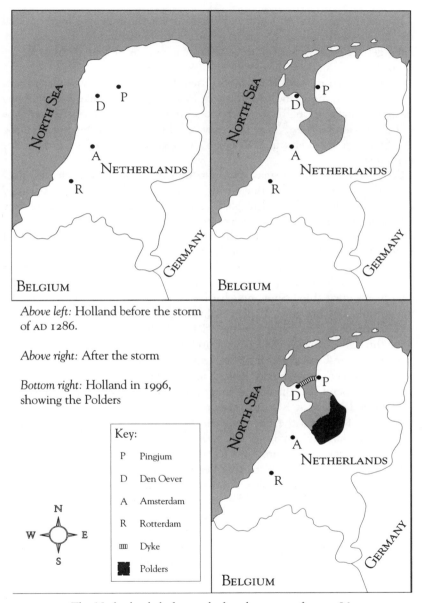

Above left: Holland before the storm of AD 1286.

Above right: After the storm

Bottom right: Holland in 1996, showing the Polders

Key:

P   Pingjum

D   Den Oever

A   Amsterdam

R   Rotterdam

▥   Dyke

◼   Polders

The Netherlands before and after the storm of AD 1286.

Rients thought and thought and felt sorry for those people from so long ago. He knew they were his great, great grandparents and he suddenly said, 'Let's get that land back so we can farm it and make our families happy again.'

'Sure, let's do it,' said Wiepkje. So these two decided to haul some rocks and dirt to the shore and to pile them in the ocean to make a dam. They wanted to make a long dam which would hold back the water. When they told their parents, Rients' dad said they could use their two big horses, Grog and Slog, on Saturdays and Wiepkje's dad gave them a long wagon for hauling stones.

Soon they had built a small dam out from the shore in a circle and they scooped the water out and the sun dried up the land. They were so happy to see good soil and decided to plant something. Wiepkje put in some nice red tulips and few yellow Dutch potatoes. Rients planted flax because that was what his dad did. Soon their little farm had beautiful red flowers mixed in with the bright blue flowers of the flax.

One day as they sat looking at their accomplishment Rients looked up and said, 'Hey look, out past our dam on the Zuyder Zee, I think it is the King in his great ship.' Sure enough there was the royal ship with its bright orange sails and big guns. It kept sailing right towards them and the kids were frightened. Soon they saw their King, William the Third, looking at them through a spyglass. He landed and walked up to them. They bowed and curtsied and wondered if he was going to wreck their dam.

King William looked and looked at the dam and said to the Royal Messenger, 'Send me the Royal Engineer right now, quickly, because we want to find out what is going on here.'

Both the King and the Engineer asked the children what they had done and the King said, 'Do not be afraid.' So Rients explained how he and Wiepkje had tried to get some more land for their country, the Netherlands. The Royal Engineer said to the King that here was a great idea and they certainly could use more land. Of course the King saw that these two children had invented a very good thing and he called for his Royal Flag Bearer to bring the biggest flag they had on his ship. King William then put a pole and the flag into the garden and said this new land would be called 'The First Polder'.

When the King went back to his castle he called all his loyal subjects to come and hear about a brand new idea invented by two Fries children from Pingjum. He said he wanted a very long dam or dike to be built across the Zuyder Zee from Pingjum to Den Oever and everyone in The Netherlands could work on it.

The good King forgot about one thing and that was – money. There was not enough money to build it and he waited for many years to get the money.

During this time the two children grew and grew. Wiepkje became more beautiful all the time. She had long blond hair and a cute little nose and she knew lots of things about the home and fields. Of course Rients was tall and strong and he remembered what he had said to his dog Woopsy about getting married. So he asked Wiepkje if she would marry him and she said she would like that.

After a while, in 1905, another happy thing happened – they had a little baby boy whom they named Tjepke after his grandfather. When this boy finally got to be eighteen, in 1923, enough money had been obtained and the great dike was started. All the men in the country came with their horses, trucks, shovels and wagons and they hauled rocks for years.

Tjepke worked hard but one day he said to his dad and mum, 'I want to go to Canada and get a different job,' so in 1925 he went and found a job in Turner Valley in Alberta. A lot of people could not pronounce his name so he changed it to a new Canadian name, Charlie. Now much time has passed and we find his great-granddaughter living in Cochrane – who could that be?

The Dutch people continued to work after Tjepke (Charlie) left and finally finished the Great Dike across the Zuyder Zee. Today they have made some huge polders and many thousands of farmers work on the new land which has been taken back from the sea.

5

Tenacity

MOSQUITOES . . . tall reeds . . . water . . . and stuck to boot. How were we to get out of this predicament? Why had we taken such a chance with elderly lives and precious people on board? Would we ever survive the coming night and reach the safety of the Moose Lake Post? Well, let's struggle on and try our utmost.

It seemed so exciting when after Carol's supper Jock said, 'Carol, the lake is pretty calm so I'll take our visitors out for a spin in the speed boat.' But before this you must know the setting for this adventure.

It had started with some sentimental musings by aunts Dorothy and Hilda in July 1989. They had suggested that we take a trip to their birthplace at Moose Lake, Northern Manitoba. They had memories of such places as 'across the Portage', lobstick trees, lake shore and of the old native Indians. And of course we all wanted to see the cairn erected on their exact birthplace – now a small clearing in the bushland. So the group at the Moose Lake dinner table that night consisted of Dorothy, Hilda and Donald, the elders of the Lamb clan. Jock and Carol McAree, Vi and Don Crane and Large Black Dog made up the remainder. Dog was a very quiet and docile but overly friendly fellow of some advanced age.

There we were, all full of talk and a sense of adventure. The very mention of a spray-filled ride on the vast lake met with instant enthusiasm. The evening was just like that of 1912 when life was so full of good things.

We leapt to the tasks of filling gas tank, getting pole and paddle, pushing boat into lake. Excitement was mounting. Jock was pilot, Dot pointer of interesting places and Hilda arranger of seating. Dog was on board under feet.

Being a warm evening Hilda, Vi and Dorothy were in light summer dresses and footwear. Donald, Jock and Don were also clad in a cavalier manner for such an outing.

Off we went straight out, heading east. What fun!

Presently Dorothy and Hilda agreed in saying, 'Let's head up Moose Creek.' No sooner said than done and Jock cranked hard to starboard and we careered into said creek.

Now a short word about said creek. It was a nice size as creeks go, being about forty feet wide, of adequate depth flowing from the Summerberry river into Moose Lake. Its path was sinuous through marshland, tall seven-foot reeds and breeding grounds for birds of infinite variety. A smaller stream, Sturgeon Creek, entered the main stream from the east but it was quite narrow, hidden in the reeds and a bit uncharted – and I suppose you would consider it unsafe.

Jock was an expert on manoeuvring the craft so as to keep us all gasping in the pure fresh air. Dog was nose to breeze. Well, to give us the ultimate thrill Jock abruptly swung into Sturgeon Creek, the one that held ominous forebodings. We flew across the water, all amazed at the vegetation, when suddenly, rounding a sharp bend, we ran full steam ahead onto a sandbar and mudflat. Our ship was aground.

We had been dealt a dastardly blow. The boat was about fifteen feet from either bank – if such a bank did exist under the reeds and grasses. After a muster to action stations all was found to be OK with the ship. The passengers reported no injuries and Dog was fine but a bit concerned. Pelicans flew overhead and a million mosquitoes settled onto our poor unprotected bodies. Some laughs were heard, briefly, until someone said, 'We better get out of this mess before nightfall or we will end up quite bloodless.'

Aunts Dorothy and Hilda on the west shore of Moose Lake. Moose and Sturgeon Creeks are to the left.

Now the reader will have an inkling of the great predicament. The skipper tried to back up, then attempted rapid forward and back movements. To no avail. We were STUCK. All this time we were swatting mosquitoes, having forgotten the circling pelicans and beautiful setting sun. Oh yes, the precursor of darkness was stirring.

Ah! of course, paddles and pole were the answer. Straightaway the two relatives, Donald and Don, said they could easily paddle and push to assist the spinning propeller, which by the way was churning up the sand and mud and depositing it nicely around our hull.

Now then, to action. Donald paddled the port side while Don poled the depths for a footing upon which to push on the starboard. The ladies swung their attention from one side to the other, tennis match style. Their frantic, swatting efforts to keep the insects at bay added to the illusion of a cheering section at Wimbleton.

Don decided to plunge into the muddy current to save the precious cargo, including Dog. Off came his pants, mainly to prevent his wallet being soaked. Over he went in his shorts; he slipped into the water, mud and sand, grasped the gunnels and pushed.

Donald likewise leapt out opposite and you can now see the awesome power of the combined motor and manpower! With full throttle and a rocking motion the ship swung towards the shore but was soon mired again.

Jock yelled, 'Can you ladies and dog reach the shore and get out?' If they could then our draught and weight would be less.

The reader will remember the frightful nature of the surroundings. The marsh extended for countless acres bordering the lake and was drained by many rivulets. Shallow water held reeds, tall spear-like grasses and decaying, foul smelling debris with no defined base. Muskrats had burrowed through the mess and treacherous tunnels held hidden perils if stepped upon. Their 'push-ups' or little houses provided the only semi-solid footing for wading humans. This was mosquito heaven!

Nevertheless our two aunts (eighty-six and eighty-four) together with Vi gingerly crawled off the bow into this morass. (Dog abstained.) With their scantily shod feet they made their way through the swamp and the clouds of mosquitoes. Each step penetrated at least ten inches into the tangle.

Finally they found a spot under the towering reeds where they could at least stand still without sinking. This was a heroic endeavour. Can you imagine these three ladies in water and muck embracing each other, warding off the monsters with futile brushing? Wet and exhausted they hung on.

Meanwhile back at the ship, what with pushing from each side and with full throttle, the craft was at last free to sail away. But what about the ladies? The men looked back and by listening to slaps, screams and squishy noises they thought them to be about two hundred feet away. How they ever managed to walk, slap and remain in good spirits was a wonder. It can probably be attributed to their hardy upbringing and determined natures.

By this time darkness was threatening but the boat crept cautiously along the pseudo-shoreline and a rescue was made. Everything was again shipshape. The two river rats covered with mud, the three dishevelled ladies all covered with welts, the shaking dog and an unscathed pilot set out carefully cruising down the winding channel. Moose Creek prompted a sigh of relief and the broad, safe lake was hailed with a cheer.

Approaching the wharf, Dog noticed a concerned Carol waving, and alerted our bedraggled group. Following a change of clothes, hot tea and baking soda (welt relief) the event was relived. If the group had been stranded overnight in such a place it would have ended in disaster. However with thankful hearts it was deemed a grand adventure. No bad effects – the aunts and Donald are now ninety-five, ninety-three and eighty-two and all is well in Lamb Land.

6

The Intransigent Snowmobile

ONCE IN A LONG TIME SOMETHING HAPPENS which, while true, is usually dismissed as being part of a tall story. Such was the case in telling of the incredible runaway snowmobile. Most acquaintances to whom this story was verbally related nodded their heads and cast sly glances which implied that I was prevaricating (again?) and it was with this in mind that the following facts are put forth for your judgement.

As the old ditty says "Twas on a cold and frosty winter's morn' and the crew was getting ready for an experimental seismic survey on the polar ice. They had left their frigid digs in the skid camp and were to proceed further northward over the vast expanse of ice. They were then to set up instruments to obtain a few recordings. Snowmobiles towed overloaded sleds with food, cables, propane and dynamite while the helpers, dressed like overstuffed mummies, trudged behind pushing equipment over ice ridges. Overhead flew a small helicopter and in it sat 'the chief' in the opulence which he so richly deserved!

So the crew finally stopped at a fluttering flag – the spot chosen by the chief (of course). Looking around they saw endless ice, some areas as smooth as glass and some rough and snow covered. Several sinuous, icy pressure ridges wrapped around the site like coiled pythons and the feeling of desolation crept into their hearts. The sun peeked out on the horizon about 11.30 a.m. but would retreat at 1.30 p.m. seemingly defeated by the cold. This desperately cold air carried the eerie, cracking ice sounds which swept across the desert.

The chief descended. With grotesque bloated arms he pointed and through a cloud of steam some words spurted forth. Immediately some bundled-up forms unloaded the sleds and then laid cables in various patterns. Another snort from the over-dressed chief and snowmobiles were readied.

Alas, one magnificent green vehicle stalled. Serious problem. If engines were shut down even for a short while, starting was nearly impossible. Time was important.

A group assembled around the machine and a gasoline can appeared from

The big green machine prior to its wild ride. Don walking on the right. Note the windblown shrub anchored in the ice as a marker. The red flag blew away.

underneath a distended body. With a full tank, proper throttle and choke, the frantic starting procedure was tried again and again. What could be wrong? Then the chief rolled into view and with adept manipulation of the controls and with plenteous help the green monster leapt to life. Surprise and wonder . . . it was in gear, but no one was in the driver's seat!

With a tremendous roar, at full throttle, big green thundered off over the ice. The crew miraculously began shedding layer upon layer of feathers and wool and what should appear but a bunch of robust men, eager to subdue the green dragon. But the machine was an intransigent runaway careering eastward.

It seemed that the steering arm was in such a position as to allow it to travel straight ahead and that meant it would reach Victoria Island or maybe some other remote place. But no, did you see that? Runaway had bounced over a small pressure ridge and the steering was altered. It headed north. The other machines were remobilized with the idea of forming a posse to give chase. However a heavily laden horse cannot outrun a wild mustang and the Green One would probably outdistance such a pack. Just then fate interposed and the machine's course was changed by another small ice ridge.

'Look out,' cried the posse leader, 'The thing is coming back, right at us.'

A wild scatter ensued and the racer sped past and bounced crazily onto a new tack.

It became obvious that present tactics were not at all suitable. Then an ingenious helper suggested the helicopter could be more effective in the chase so the pilot entered the fray and with the strongest man he took off. Two valiant heroes with only a small helicopter and a fifty-foot rope were to attack the monster.

With a spiral lift off they swung to the west and soon were tracking the beast. Strongman, well buckled and unafraid, leaned out of the open door holding a large noose in his hand. With tricky flying skills the whirlybird followed the runaway and the noose was gently hooked over the steering bar. Again alas. No further plans had been thought of and the bird was anchored to the beast by a muscular right arm. All went well until their course changed again, abruptly. The multi-thousand dollar bird was nearly brought to ground in a fatal crash but the skilled pilot regained control, swerving hither and yon.

The whup, whup of the rotor blades and the screaming engine drowned out the pilot's frantic words – 'Let go . . . let go of the rope. The rope!' followed by some more descriptive phrases common among such groups. Strongman, being somewhat unaware of impending danger, was reluctant to let go.

He bellowed, 'I'll throw a half hitch over the 'copter strut.'

However seeing the pilot's mouthed expletives he finally dropped the rope. With the lessened weight the 'copter surged upward, regained its composure and returned to the red flag, thoroughly defeated.

Meantime, the raging mustang was returning again to the huddled posse. A second strongman had an idea! With a fair sized, full propane tank held high above his head he waited. The mobile was coming back and as it flew past he hurled the tank, hoping to bend its steering bar into a cramped position or upset it. The tank succeeded in smashing the windshield and bounced away.

However, another quick-witted helper, the ultimate hero of the day, saw the rope snaking behind and with a mighty leap he grabbed it and disappeared in a cloud of snow.

As it happened, the rope on the steering bar redirected the green machine. It began describing large radius circles around our bruised but unrelenting hero. This rotating pair were soon joined by a second stationary snowmobile which became caught up, entering the ballet. Now with three forces swirling in concert the overheated green machine finally became entangled and overturned. Dodging the spinning tracks a final hero reached in and turned the switch. Suddenly all became ominously quiet and the awesome Arctic deadness stole in upon us.

The work site was unbelievably disorganized. Parkas, tanks, cables, instruments, food, sleds and men had gone through a hurricane and a work day was essentially in jeopardy. No appropriate labours could be done because of the laughter and reenactments of the events.

Chief, ever serious and responsible, swept his bulky arm over the scene and indeed some work was then in order. The snickers and banter continued all that day and on many occasions ever since. In retelling the saga everyone tried most conscientiously to stick to the facts so in keeping with this standard you now know the full and unabridged story of the intrepid runaway.

7

The Gathering-in

THERE WAS EXCITEMENT IN THE AIR that bright spring day in the little Outer Hebrides village. And well there might be for this was the day of the gathering-in. This was the day, indeed, for the sheep were to be located on the common and herded across the moor to their summer home on the croft. My part in this fervour was limited to spectator status and though I was in the midst of the preparations I was strangely on the fringe, largely unnoticed.

The excitement was not of the loud, raucous type found in our western Canadian cattle roundup. Rather, it showed as a sparkle in the old Scot's eye in the corner of the wee kitchen. And in the elaborate fussing by the busy mother as she made tea and talked of the individual sheep, known so well. Then it showed when the neighbours popped in and out for a two minute visit, seemingly for no reason whatsoever. The dogs, the precious, excited but obedient dogs, were leaping and crouching, obviously aware of the big day and the important part they were to play.

From out of nowhere, Angus appeared with Lady, his beautiful black and white border collie. He appeared, sat and smiled in the kindly manner so typical of the hardy ones. Angus was probably in his sixties and obviously a good friend. I was bursting with questions but in the atmosphere of restraint detected in the household, I remained calm and observed.

The Mcleod croft was on the Atlantic side of the rocky island. A modest stone house, barn and loom shed stood sentinel over the sloping croft which was the summer home of seventy ewes with their lambs. They were a grand lot. Quite small by southern standards, the Lewis sheep were extremely hardy and adaptable. In the winter however the sheep could not be sustained on the croft and they were simply turned out onto the great common or moor which covered the central part of the island. Alone, but free, several hundred ewes wandered far and wide, mixing, grazing and surviving. In the spring, before the lambs dropped, they were gently herded home, inoculated, dipped and comforted. Each bore their owner's distinctive mark – but my observation was that the real identification was under the eye of the wife, regardless of the paint.

The Gathering-in

Murdo, Angus and Lady (and I) were to search the moor this day. Lunch being prepared, we set out in the little Volvo, crowded but excited. I watched Lady with amazement as she crouched between Angus' feet. Her eyes were glued to his face and she quivered continuously. Jumping out onto the moor she froze to his left leg and anticipated his every step. It occurred to me that the entire focus of this day would be on this well-trained collie. Neither of the Scots acknowledged her presence, nor did they pat or say a word. My inclination, as a pet lover, was to do just that but again I restrained myself for the sake of harmony.

We walked over the water-sodden moor searching for ewes with a double blue cross on the left side or a black bar on the left haunch. Great hummocks of heather were interspersed on the wet peat. Now and then a rocky knoll served as a vantage point and rest stop. The several small streams promised wet crossings and soggy socks.

Suddenly Lady became detached from the leg of Angus and flowed rather than raced through the heather. I raised my glasses and saw far ahead two sheep with blue crosses. Obviously Angus had spotted them and at a signal Lady had erupted. Murdo was excited but outwardly placid as we watched Lady speed along. She stopped to look back and at that moment Angus raised his right arm which magically turned her in that direction. She approached the defensive animals, crouched and stared them into submission. We covered the four hundred yards to this little group and Murdo calmly took charge and herded our first catch along with us. Easy as pie, I thought.

Continuing northwards we scanned the hills and vales for the elusive woollies and in no time found a real challenge for Lady. On the lea side of a hill, one half mile to the west, we saw six sheep with various markings, one of which seemed to bear a black bar.

At a signal, Lady streaked off at an oblique angle and soon was crouching in a small vale out of sight of the sheep, awaiting instructions. At each wave and occasional whistle she responded and approached the group. It was important to respect the pregnant ewes: to prevent a stampede and to provide rest periods when herding. Lady instinctively knew this and gently moved among the six and, using Angus's long distance instructions, isolated the black bar. Then unbelievably she walked the selected one back to our small flock. It was magnificent to watch.

I felt somewhat more useful after a few hours of 'shepherding' and enjoyed lifting the weak ones over the steams.

During our short lunch break we sat on a grassy knoll with our backs against an ancient sheiling. Murdo and Angus reminisced on the old days

Several of the Lewis sheep on the moor. Taken later in the summer after the lambs were dropped.

when they inhabited this little one-roomed stone building. Again the stories of peat cutting and herring fishing were related and all was peaceful. This naturally lead to dozing and the four of us were quite uncommunicative for twenty minutes.

We found poor Booey in a dreadful state. Lady had located her mired in a muddy stream out of our sight and had refused to leave her. We therefore waded the quarter mile to the disaster site and carried the poor weak thing to high ground. Booey, you see, was about to have her first-born a bit early and she still had three miles to walk to our rendezvous point. The growing convoy was now proceeding at a very slow rate but many more were to join us before dark.

Lady continued to stare with adoration at Angus and she seemed inexhaustible. She ran, selected and herded the sturdy ones and the stubborn ones and the old ones and the young ones. Once, while she forded another steam we talked of her abilities and pedigree. Angus had trained her from a pup as he had with her mother and grandmother. She had gradually replaced her forebears and would be the principle actor on these outings for many years to come.

We trudged along in like manner until we noticed Murdina waiting at our rendezvous with the little Volvo. Suddenly she was amongst us excitedly handling each ewe. 'Och, you poor wee dears', 'Oh my blessed babies', 'How weak you little darlings are.' We bundled little Booey into the boot and another into the front seat and continued down the dirt trail homewards. The stronger ones trotted along behind under Lady's watchful eye.

Rest and a wee dram restored my legs enough to take a turn through the barn. Murdina was picking ticks, fondling and feeding a mash to the precious ones and all was well. Angus, upon leaving us, let his hand fall to the head of Lady and a restrained, affectionate patting was noted. Then as they strode homewards I heard some kind cooing words and saw certain loving glances pass between the two.

8

Mauja

A LL SNOW IS NOT JUST 'SNOW'. As our far Northern people have observed, for centuries, there are very many varieties and each has a name. For instance *kinirtaq*, in the Inuit language is damp, compact, snow; *kataqattarnaq* is hard crusted snow and the other eighteen or twenty types describe, in a word, conditions critical to their existence. However, the snow that brought us to exhaustion was the fateful *mauja* – the deep, soft, fluffy snow on the ground.

During the building of the Alaska Highway, a series of landing strips had been hurriedly slashed out of the wild bush-land of northern British Columbia. These were not the kind suitable for anything but the most rugged of airplanes of the era, and were hardly ever used by anyone after the road was finished in 1942. Still they remained, beside the gravel highway, being overgrown by scrub brush and sometimes covered, in winter, by – *mauja*.

During a particular winter twenty years later, we had plenty of the deep fluffy stuff and by February it was about four feet deep in most places. The *mauja* had fallen softly in the absence of wind and was partially supported by the long grass and scrub willow and new-growth spruce below. A poetic person would have been in raptures seeing a little airstrip alone in the wilderness wrapped in such a snug blanket.

We, however, were not in the rapturous state looking down from our little Cessna plane that miserable February morning. George and I had been scouting the forest to select the best route for the bulldozers as they struggled along making a new trail. Our crew was waiting for help, far away in a ravine, and we felt the pressure to hurry.

The old bush pilot, smoking as usual, was banking right and left according to our hand motions. Steeply right so George could examine the bush, then to the left for me. Back and forth, up and down. I had had no breakfast because of the upchuck risk but even so my stomach was growing more angry with every dip and dive. George was flipping maps in the air – first the top was west, then south, then northeast – to make it easier to make his fancy marks.

It was at this point that we appeared near an old, *mauja*-covered airstrip. The pilot had to relieve himself and said, 'I am going down for a minute and we will be back up in five.' Well, thought I, not a bad idea; it will be quite refreshing.

A steep bank and a swooping downward glide brought us over the south end of the very short strip. Small plane, no problem! We touched the top of the snow with the Cessna's skis and immediately stirred up an angry cloud which swirled and tumbled beside and behind us. George peeped up from under his inverted map and the pilot chewed hard on his stubby cigar butt. I thought the landing was much like a belly-flop from a high board into a pool.

Decelerating at a stunning rate we ploughed a wide swath through the snow, underlying grass and twigs but even at this rate we came abruptly to the end of the so-called strip. The skis were buried, as were parts of the struts. The lighter tail piece was still visible and we could push one door open with ease so out we jumped. Our refreshing interlude commenced!

The pilot seemed to be unfazed and said, 'The snow is deeper this year; I landed on this strip only four years ago and it was a snap. Let's just tramp down the snow a bit and we can carry the tail around 180 degrees and take off the way we came in.'

We tramped and grunted on the circle selected but the resentful *mauja* would not pack down because, by definition, it was fluffy. Using our feet and legs as shovels, a small clearing was finally made. Tail turned, and the three of us hopped in, ready for take-off. The propeller raged, snow swirled and we moved, but only so far as the edge of our small cleared circle.

Being on the ground the plane's radio refused to reach anyone for help so we returned to the job of kicking snow to make a path.

It was fruitless to try to push *mauja* away in order to make a path long enough for take-off. The dead grass and small branches entangled around legs and feet. Luckily it was about minus 35 degrees with no wind so our sweaty bodies balanced out against the cold, crispy air. But our exhaustion and the cooling of the engine were factors to be considered.

Suddenly George looked up and pointed a quivering finger to a leaning pole between us and the sparsely used roadway. A sagging wire swung away from a box on the pole. Could it be an ancient telephone box?

The old highway maintenance crews had not had effective radios in those days and used a hastily constructed telephone line on occasion for emergencies. We had an emergency so off we tramped to try it. *Mauja* resisted because she felt victory within her grasp. We battled back and reached the broken box. Yes, there was an old phone, dry and ready.

'Hello, operator, does this thing work?'

'Of course,' replied an angelic voice, 'what is your trouble?'

We were puffing so hard and so stunned that she thought we were drunk, and so early in the day too.

Hooking up to Pat's office we found out that the dozers, crew and drills were all on standby, waiting for our instructions. This was an expensive issue so George waded back to the plane, returned with maps and gave our sketchy scouting results. A huge snow-plough truck was dispatched to rescue us and late in the evening the war between *mauja* and technology was over.

During the long hungry wait I sat on a stump looking at our adversary. She was beautiful in a poetic sort of way. Her pure white dress, made up of millions of large crystals, sparked in the oblique rays from the sun. Each little curve over underlying brush, hummocks and fallen trees enhanced her voluptuous contours. At a touch she changed her form and retreated, desirable but sacred. It seemed such a pity that in another month or two she would melt away and might not be attracted to this spot again for decades. We never returned.

9

Twin Otter

How do you clean house living in a tent? That was the problem. The solution was found in the statement that the President was due for a visit and you darn well make things neat and clean. Yes, there was a bit of a mess in the corner near the tent flap and maybe the bed should be made. Several other things could be rearranged if one really was forced into it. After tending to these chores the old green tent did look presentable and my chest swelled with pride.

The tents were pitched on a rare, flat delta plain near an unnamed fiord on Northern Ellesmere Island. This Canadian Arctic island was the scene of an exploration survey in the very short summer of 1969. Arriving in mid-June we had pounded tent pegs into the frozen mud and laughingly teased the cook that the permafrost was only 1,500 feet deep, but his cook-tent would be well anchored anyway.

The important visit to our ten-tent village was to include the Pres. and various chiefs of lesser importance. They were to fly over the northern tip of the island, swing over the prospective objectives and then land at our camp for an hour visit, to lunch and have a picture taking ceremony. Some of the crew members actually shaved and one even put on a shirt we had never seen before.

The cook fired up his propane stove and turned out some overcooked muffins and some hardtack cookies. The crew was on hand, having given up half of the work day. We were ready.

Out of the north came a marvellous Twin Otter airplane, the workhorse of the islands. Banking gracefully it examined the frozen (?) mud flat much like a wary Canada goose views a barley field. Our little Beaver aircraft was poised on the edge of the campsite and had not been on a trip for a week.

Seeing this, the pilot gently lowered the Twin Otter onto the ground and, as was the custom, came to a speedy stop. Through swinging doors the pilot jumped and positioned a wee ladder for his important passengers. Down they came, one by one, shaking hands and full of smiles on this their day of perks.

Gus was the first to notice the impending troublesome thing about the plane. It was gently sinking into the mud. How could that be? But by this time, all the potentates had retired to the kitchen and were mouthing the muffins and holding up a cookie or two. The visit progressed and numerous pictures were snapped. First the Pres. with the cook, then with a chief holding up a northern rock. etc., etc. Finally the hour was up, time to get back to Resolute, catch the commercial airliner and return south.

'Good-bye all.' 'Thanks for the hospitality.' 'See you in the fall.'

Lots of handshakes and more smiles. Gus, however, had pulled me by the arm, scurried around the corner of a tent and looked with wonder at the big, powerful, heavy plane. You guessed it. The wheels were down thirteen inches into the mud resting on the underlying permafrost. During our two weeks stay the ever present sun had done a job on our reliable permafrost, thawing the top layer.

Around the corner came the pilot, Pres. and chiefs. Confidently both engines were started; they warmed and exerted their fearsome power. The tail rose in expectation but all three wheels remained embedded. That plane could back up, maybe, but no, it stayed put. Juggling and jumping on the outstretched wings was fruitless so everyone alighted and stood around suggesting all sorts of fantastic solutions.

The tent camp on the unnamed fiord with the Beaver parked near the fuel dump. Notice the lack of vegetation.

Pres. then cried out, 'We have missed our CPA flight so let us stay for dinner.'

The cook blanched and scurried off to the pit which was our cold storage depot. Conversations were reopened as we waited for the sumptuous meal being prepared. Six o'clock came, then seven and finally at seven-thirty the dining tent was filled.

After the meal, which tasted pretty fair owing to the great hunger sauce, we decided to put some of our precious plywood under the wheels and it would just ride up and out. It did not. Next came the great idea of the rope attached to the tail. Eleven members of the group then pulled while the props roared in reverse. In spite of some danger that the plane might run over the group we kept up the pressure. Again to no avail: it was in too deep and was heavily laden.

At that time, early July, the sun was quite energetic and stayed up all night, tricking us into thinking we still had to work. By midnight, though, we were weary and the Pres. decided to stay the night. Yikes! Where to billet the brass?

The Twin Otter with reserve pitch propellers being assisted by eleven stalwart helpers.

I was chosen to house the Pres. (cleanest tent!) and gave him my spare safari cot, the one with the stained canvas bottom.

It is one thing to greet the Pres. smilingly when met on the office elevator, but very difficult to engage in idle chit-chat while undressing side by side standing on one foot. He was obviously upset with the world and it was pleasant when he turned his back and tried to get comfortable.

After breakfast of nicely crisped pancakes we had a plan. All six shovels were plied to dig mud and make channels in front of the wheels. That mud was sticky and heavy but with a large workforce the paths were cleared down to frost level.

Thankfully, owing to its exceptional power, the plane needed only a short runway and that is what it got from us. Two hours later we gazed upward at the departing Twin Otter and its growling passengers who were not looking forward to another stay-over in Resolute. Our group cheered and danced about; at last we could get back to real work.

10

Nose Power

WHAT A WONDERFUL REMINDER of past events is the power of smell. Our noses remember objects, places and of course people. For instance, even now, when I smell purple concord grapes I am transported back to the 1940s and our village general store. With closed eyes do you recall the distinctive smell of poplar buds in the springtime; the smell of a damp cellar; fresh bread, brown sugar, horses or steam from a locomotive?

Unconsciously I became aware of my surroundings at a very early age with this very welcome sense. Today I have noticed several of my grandchildren sniffing a bag, pot, food or even a person to reinforce their evaluation of each thing. I am happy for them.

I had reached my teen years in 1941 and was becoming quite relaxed in the smell department. All odours were interesting and no smell was particularly 'bad', even that cloud wafting up from Uncle L's pig pen. True it was not nice but that was what pigs smelled like and it was accepted, not abhorred. I understood the smells of my world and was confident, happy and relaxed.

Now it happened that we had a hockey team complete with skates, sticks and one puck. Mr Newlove our coach looked us over one day and said, 'Each one of you must have shin-pads (probably a part of a catalogue) on each leg, and mitts to wear. The big out of town game between us, Valparaiso, and Arpsville is tomorrow and Mr M will be taking us in his van.'

Wow! We loved that van. It was essentially a big box on sleigh runners, pulled by his black stallion Ben and young Bess, his best horses. Two long board seats flanked the inside walls and it even had an old gas-can stove to burn poplar wood. Eleven players and three friends squeezed onto the board seats with all our sticks thrown in the aisle and off we went to Arpsville.

On the way home, in the twilight interior, I was packed in between Ray H and Shirley J who had come along for the excitement. I sat knowing that Mr M was there because of the 'Old Chum' tobacco he smoked. Steamy horse smells came through the rein slot. Someone was eating a baloney sandwich. Familiar, reassuring smells.

As I leisurely turned my head towards Shirley I was struck by a lightning

Valparaiso hockey team in 1939, three years before the entrapment. Ray 3rd from the right; Don beside him with the cap on.

bolt! What was that sensational smell? It was not in my memory bank. I felt an excitement totally foreign.

Leaning a bit closer to her it was confirmed and I thought to myself, 'Shirley smells so good. It is not perfume, sweat, soap or anything I have ever known.' It seemed to be coming from her nose!

I sat mulling things over, feeling a strange attraction to my near companion. Thinking back to last August I found a simple corollary which seemed to be familiar. In Mr M's corral I had seen Ben and Bess nose to nose, breathing deeply. Ben was acting crazy and out of character. He stomped, swung his head back and forth and almost danced. Now I felt a strange urge to breathe more deeply. Was I going crazy?

Shirley sat quietly and I thought she was nodding off to sleep so I cautiously bent closer and whiffed. There was something mighty attractive about her. Why? I had often played with her and others and had treated her as one of my buddies. Not now. I had never noticed how pretty her mouth and eyes were. She seemed to be so perfect that I would not dare touch her.

My mum often said, 'You are my precious one and I love you.' It was nice to hear and love meant just that so this smell business was not, obviously, connected with love. But yet it was more than friendship – what did it mean? The next day I ambled near other girls but no such sensation overcame me. They just did not smell special. Lorna, Mable and Myrtle smelled just like all the boys.

It was torture and I could not bear to talk about it to Dad, Mum or Ray. Finally after an obscure hint to Ray he looked quite understanding and mentioned that his other friend, Dan, had felt funny around a girl.

Ray's query was, 'Do your nipples hurt?'

'No, but they sure are tender this year. I wish I knew why!'

Don with the bike and a passenger on the handy crossbar.

Apparently Ray had used up all his anatomical knowledge and the conversation swung to hockey again. Still, every time I even saw Shirley I was overwhelmed by strange emotions. Surely God had planted a time bomb in me and it was ticking. I made sure she was unaware of these feelings. She and my sister Norma (who, by the way, smelled normal) were often together and this made my juggling act even more difficult.

Dad kept up our conversations but sometimes he had a bigger smile than usual.

One day he said, 'Are you OK?'

Could he have known what I was going through? Did he know? Oh, it was awful and I resolved to be more nonchalant, but there was Shirley standing across the street.

Winter progressed and with the Christmas excitement I became slightly more at ease. After my fourteenth birthday in February I had overcome my shyness and bravado manner around Shirley and soon conquered, forever, my emotions regarding her. Besides her eyes seemed less attractive now and she sure was skinny. What was the big deal anyhow?

'Now,' I said to my big dog, Lobo, 'now I am free from those strange feelings.'

He agreed and was glad to romp in the snow again. He smelled good also, except when he was too wet.

Spring came, bicycles came out and we (boys and girls) had great fun riding over rubber ice on the slough. Slushy snowball fights, meeting the train and general rough-housing was the ultimate fun. After one such group outing I offered to give Myrtle a ride home on my bike's cross-bar. Going east on the gravel road our heads bumped together and . . . Oh no! Myrtle smelled just the way Shirley used to smell. I was ensnared and doomed for the rest of the summer.

The Day I Ate Too Much

W E ALL TRY TO BE CONSERVATIVE in our eating habits, do we not? No? Well then, do we try to eat sensibly? No? How about delectable meat, roast potatoes and sweets? Are they so tough to resist? Yes. Yes indeed, and I must tell you how I really intended to be modest in my food intake on a great journey to Eastern Europe in 1986 – and how I failed. This decision for moderation came about after my fellow travellers and I had been treated to such wonderful hospitality and such good food. It happened in this manner.

Poland in 1986, still under the powerful Communist thumb, was an austere and downtrodden state. The watchful eye of the government had enforced subjection on the people and their natural fun-loving characteristic had been beaten down. To me in ultra-free Canada it seemed that Poland was very depressing. However as things turned out I was to change my mind with a great leap.

In spite of suppression, Communists had encouraged university research which resulted in two doctors having discovered and developed a new method of oil exploration. We geophysicists had been sent over to see if it had value for Canada.

We were briefed in Warsaw and Krakow and then took a long overland journey to Eastern Poland to have the doctors describe the equipment and tell how it worked. During all this time we enjoyed our hosts and were struck by the fact that they were subtly resistant to Communist ideals but in the presence of the overlords were silent. When we Canadians arrived, the state sanctioned full entertainment and relaxed quotas. So this day was special for them also as they ordinarily could not participate in such abundance and festivities. Quite a change from the long food lines.

At our delayed Krakow breakfast one interpreter said, 'You must eat a BIG breakfast because we will travel far today.' (200 km!)

And what a breakfast it was. First a thick gruel, fruit and a delicious fish concoction. Then bacon and eggs, potatoes and thick dark bread. It was about three times my usual fare but we were to travel far!

Lunch at the Pastewnik restaurant. Vodka in the foreground.

The huge van opened to let in the seven Canadians, two Polish doctors, three interpreters and, not to be forgotten, two communist watchdogs. The latter were sober, stiff, attentive and in the way. Every comment by the guides was noted by them. The scientists were not party members and held a careful disdain for the 'spies'. Our first stop was at the headquarters of a politician where we sat in an absolutely lavish office, not at all like the one room, one table office of the university scientists.

A bureaucrat, opening a decorated desk, withdrew the choicest vodka to which we all paid homage with etched glasses. So early and so soon after being stuffed the liquor seemed a bit heavy but following custom we had to have another.

The 'boss' was most affable towards us, telling of the great strides they had made in governing Poland. But to the doctors he was very rude; embarrassing and humiliating them right before our eyes. We felt uneasy but they had been treated this way for years and sat in stoic silence. We felt that the day was going to be long and tough.

Once in our van, however, everyone relaxed, and jokes and laughter, which cannot be held down, bounced around.

'The optimist learns Chinese but the pessimist learns Russian.' Ha, Ha, Ha . . . Whoops, a slip of the lip and the 'spy' did not smile.

Our path led east from Krakow through many towns with unpronounceable names such as Wieliczka and Ropzyce. They pointed out farmers ploughing with one horse and a hand held plough. Also noted were piles of sand, brick and lumber in various quantities in front of the small, essentially wrecked farmhouses. The war-torn farmers had not yet recovered from the devastation and were accumulating building materials slowly. The size of these piles denoted the status of each family.

Stopping two hours after breakfast we arrived at the Pastewnik (Shepherd) restaurant in isolated farm country. It was a masterful lunch. Sitting at the long table we had a waiter for every two people. He held two bottles of Zyntink vodka which kept coming and coming.

Suddenly a doc stood up, dashed black pepper onto his vodka, pointed to one of us and, with a hearty Polish voice uttered a toast, 'Na Sdrovia.'

'Na Sdrovia,' all chanted. Chug-a-lug, down went fourteen pepper-flecked glasses, now empty. It behoved the toasted one then to honour someone else to whom we all quaffed a glass.

'Na Sdrovia' . . . 'Na Sdrovia' . . .

On my breakfast-laded stomach this was getting a bit much but we all sank or swam together and good manners demanded we toast again and again.

The arrival of wine and a savory cabbage and ham borscht relieved us of toasting. The thick, brown soup was fantastic and I finished my bowl only to look up an see my waiter's arm present me with another bowl – this was a thick, red beet borscht. Lovely. An interesting platter next set in front of each man contained a mound of raw steak tartare in the middle, surrounded by bowls of raw egg, peppers, onions, mustard and cayenne. Very filling and substantial. The main course of succulent wild boar with crackling skin and browned fat sent shivers of delight up my spine. What the heck, we were to travel far today and I finished it with all the accompanying brown potatoes, melon and veggies.

'Now is the time to quit,' I said to my near companion who nodded weakly.

But no, now came the heavy, steaming pudding covered with an exquisite caramel sauce. We were very, very full; but ever onward. Topping it off with a Polish sweet wine and vodka chaser we sat stupidly looking at each other. We still had to travel far.

No so far did we travel before coming to a dense forest where another

The picnic in the forest near Jaroslaw.

group had sacrificed their precious rations for our enjoyment. Rolling out of the van we saw a picnic site and the large, burning fire pit. A bench with vodka and black buns was ready and long pointed saplings stood primed for the roasting. Large, savoury, Kielbasaa sausages lay about and some exuberant person pushed back the coals to reveal large potatoes wrapped in corn husks, well baked. Seeing the expectant expression on the Polish faces we realized that a new feast was being thrust upon us.

Oh! the pain. Our stomachs, still bubbling with eggs, boar, pudding, et al, almost refused the offerings but were over-ruled by the mind which argued for acceptance. After all we were guests and deserved the best.

The familiar greeting, 'Na Sdrovia, Na Sdrovia' echoed through the forest.

A doctor announced, 'We are very close to Jaroslaw and close to the USSR; do not stroll eastward!'

After a short walk we came upon the working crew. Staring at the instruments, cables and electrodes in a fuzzy haze we listened to the doctors explain the operation. They, by the way, seemed capable of withstanding such an onslaught of food and vodka. The fresh air helped to clear our minds and the hour came to an end with all professing to have grasped the principles.

Since it was only about 4 p.m., a scheduled trip to a museum brought us to the Palace at Lansuit, 60 km to the west. This sixteenth century palace had been closed during and after the war but was later opened as a museum. Very few visitors and almost no foreigners reached this remote spot. The 'spies' gave a good lecture on the glories of the Red Regime and how Poland had benefited through the efforts of the Party. Dutifully listened to by all, the doors were then swept open and after a few rich canapés we viewed the magnificent of Polish past.

Shortly a voice resounded, 'All Canadian visitors and guides are to retire to the grand dining hall.'

'What for?' whispered a terrified companion to me.

I jokingly said, 'For the grand banquet, I suppose.'

What fateful words! There was the magnificent banquet table, the high back, carved chairs, the numerous waiters with the familiar bottle in each hand. Shrinking backwards, no end of excuses entering my mind. However our indestructible doctors and guides pressed forward, almost dragging these fragile visitors, until we found the seats of honour.

You guessed it! The toasts seemed more numerous, the appetizers more decorative and interesting, the first and second courses more varied and tempting. But at this time it would have been so easy to resist temptation were it not for the eager and expectant appearance of our most hospitable companions. Expensive wines and elaborate desserts now faded to a blur as I sat looking at my plates and glasses.

After the long repast, sitting in the van for our return, I desperately wanted to sag into the corner. Our hosts however felt the urge to sing, but to sing the rousing prewar ditties and folk songs was to risk censure by the spies. So a few politically correct songs were started, but half heartedly, and soon faded away. Someone passed around bottles of Polish Zywiec beer and the hearty ones carried on.

The inspection mission ended at our hotel. In broken Polish we yelled out, '*Dziekuje, dziekuje* . . . ' 'Thank you. Thank you,' before stumbling upstairs, thoroughly defeated. The hardy Poles, with waving arms and friendly, smiling faces retired to the tavern for goodness knows what reason. I did not sleep well that night.

12

The Limestone Boulder

T HE WINTER CLASSES AT THE UNIVERSITY were finally finished and we overworked students were then released from our tormenting professors and free to find a job for the summer. The previous season, in 1949, I had had a great time working underground for four months at the Flin Flon, Manitoba copper mine. I had visions of returning to the area but really wanted a challenging, 'outdoor position' to clear my theory packed brain. Luckily I was hired as an assistant on a surface geological party which suited me to a tee. Off I went on the train to Flin Flon, found the geologists right on the main street but was astounded to learn that our leader was none other than Dr B.

Dr B was a professor at U of S and my teacher. The other students and I were quite aware that his eye had been on us all winter. Now we were to quake under his watchful eye all summer.

Our job was to assist the geologists to map rock formations on a long peninsula on the west side of Amisk lake. We read aerial maps, located outcrops, determined their distance and bearing and paced off to locate them on the ground. I, being the most junior of the group, was assigned to Dr B, and tried very hard to find the proper rock in the midst of muskeg, swamp and thick underbrush. After testing his patience for a whole week I found a beautiful greywacke outcrop at the right place and won a quiet 'good' from the doctor.

I felt that I had a good grip on this job but was shocked the next day when told that I was now to be the cook. Jerry, my fellow student, had been cooking for the camp and I naively thought he was 'the cook' for the summer.

It was soon apparent however that the students took turns at this, the lowliest job of all. Facing the little tin stove in the messy corner of an old, abandoned miner shack I thought back to my Mum and how she would attack the problem. I then decided on perserverance and experimentation so using some sacrificial potatoes, hamburger and onions I began with optimism. The first offerings were terrible and I was soon known as the "charcoal kid".

A strange quietness descended on the table when the troop of seven sat down to eat. Through the smoke I could see a resigned, stony face on the doctor's bench and then I resolved to learn more about this geological cooking business. The assistant chief was a good-natured geologist and I sought him out in the evening and confessed my sins of omission in the cooking field.

He was amused and said, 'Your black potatoes are not so black as mine were five years ago. I think I can give you a few basic lessons on how to redeem yourself.'

The tricky small, wood burning tin stove required constant care to keep the top at a reasonable temperature and the makeshift oven was a mystery of the first magnitude. However the lake trout and muskies were plentiful and with three days of helpful hints I managed to turn out a fair meal. The trouble was the crew expected another one and another and another. At my wit's end I thought that a burned steak and crispy fried potatoes might get me out of the kitchen but my nerve failed. Just then, however, it was time for cook shift change and they dragged Jerry back and I was a free man again.

I later realized that each student had been undergoing a test in all phases of life and that 'cooking' and 'finding outcrop' were parts of the grand examination.

The survey crew on Amisk lake ready to start the summer. Don 3rd from the left: His Eminence on the far right.

The Crane's Tale

One day the good leader sat on a huge granite boulder and, while I made tea with muskeg water, he actually talked to me about my future. He suggested that I study the rocks on a small peninsula, do the microscopic work and write up my findings. He would guide me and use some of my work in his own stupendous five-year mapping project. What an opportunity to make up for all those horrible things that I had put into his stomach.

However, regular work still had to be done so next week his eminence and I got into the eighteen-foot Peterborough canoe and set out on a twenty-mile trip across Amisk Lake to the south shore to check some Ordovician limestone. We arrived at the huge hundred-foot cliff and beached the canoe at the bottom while he proceeded to pick up and hammer some fragments. He said he would walk the shoreline and be back in an hour or two. As the limestone was not part of my personal project I struggled up to the top of the outcrop and sat looking out onto the lake, watching the loons.

Tiring of this inactivity I decided to toss rocks into the lake below – what a splash! I kept throwing larger and larger limestone blocks and finally found a sixty-pound boulder. It was a beauty, angular and rough. It was difficult to lift but I struggled to manhandle it to the edge. I then rolled it over the

The laden canoe moving equipment to a new campsite. Don at the outboard motor and Jerry (the cook!) in the bow. Before the Explosion.

cliff and stood horrified to see it make a direct hit on our only canoe. The front end exploded. The tea can, extra clothes and food were pulverised and imbedded into the rubble.

I glanced up from the destruction to the shoreline and was paralysed to see the Great One just approaching. After a knuckle scraping descent I trembled in front of him but was relieved to see a slight smile creep over his face and a sideways glance in my direction.

He said, 'That was a direct hit, I presume.'

Then a slight chuckle leaked out as he walked slowly up to the crumpled ship. As well as the canoe being broken the ice was melted between us as we assessed the wreckage. My profuse apologies were swept aside while he announced, much to my unbelief, 'You know, I once was young myself.'

We then loaded all the heavies into the stern, launched the canoe, sat side by side on the aft gunnel and sped, at top speed, out into Amisk. By keeping the speed at the maximum we kept the shattered bow up and set a record for the crossing.

The summer progressed and a relaxed mood descended on our little group. We shot at garbage-seeking bears; panned gold in a abandoned mine; made weekly canoe trips to town for supplies and enjoyed the great outdoors – and cooked.

13

The Dancing Lesson

THE WINTER OF '63 in northeast British Columbia was a real corker, because of the extreme cold. Nevertheless, it was a golden opportunity for the exploration crew to operate in the bush country. Muskeg was impassable in the summer heat owing to its wet and spongy nature. But in this severe winter the bog was frozen solid and the survey vehicles could get around. We, the vulnerable humans, had to put up with the bitter cold, serve the machines and suffer.

The primitive bush camp was perched on an icy river bank north of Fort Nelson, surrounded by short pines and endless snow. Daylight was a treat for a few hours each day but there the favour ended as it was work, eat and sleep day by day. The crew laboured on in a sterile atmosphere.

However into this austere world stepped an unusual, exceptional personage, Stan by name. I had just met him recently and after a few years he became one of my best friends towards whom I soon developed a spirit of true brotherly love. We just 'got along', understood each other and spent many hours talking about this and that.

He was Polish and had been raised near Krakow in an affluent family. During the war he had served as an officer in the Free Polish army across Europe and Asia minor. He had been severely wounded and given up for dead at Monte Cassino but survived to return to England for formal education. Now he was about to enter the society of the rough and tumble crew.

Further south of camp, at mile 304 on the Alaska Highway, our company had set up a service centre containing a small office and a huge heated garage under the management of Phyllis, a single secretary. All alone in a man's world, she led a lonely life to say the least. The building was filled with side-band radios, tools, supplies and a few spartan cots. But it was a haven for poor slaves to retreat to in times of emergency. It was here, in this miserable building, that the most memorable 'dancing lesson' took place.

As a small reward after crew inspection Stan said, 'Let's be off for mile 304 and have a hot shower.' Good idea! So six of us crowded into a frigid

Stan, the dancing
instructor. Picture
taken a year later
on the polar ice
near Cornwallis
Island, North
West Territories.

Land Rover, bounced for three hours over hummocks and snowbanks and
arrived at Shangri-la in mid-evening.

Phyllis, the lonesome occupant of the oasis, hailed us with, 'Boy, am I
glad to see somebody even if it is such an odoriferous group,' and immediately
pointed to the 'luxurious shower room'.

Stan, the senior member, finishing first, chatted with Phyllis and their
talk somehow swung to the subject of music. Joining this duo one by one
we fell under the spell of their conversation.

Stan was describing elegant ballroom dancing in Warsaw, Vienna and

Paris where he had danced the waltz, the gavotte and beautiful cotillions. While talking he involuntary bounced up, his arms swung unbidden to the dance position and his humming became hypnotic. A silence then descended on our motley group and we sat, fascinated.

Then very quietly a small feminine voice broke the reverie stating, 'I have a few good records. Would you like to hear them?'

Instantly Stan turned and with an expectant, happy smile said, 'Strauss? Do you have Strauss?'

Phyllis opened a plywood cupboard and there were an old record player and many long-play, 33 rpm, vinyl records, several of which were classical. Stan leaped to the record player, found Strauss, and gently lowered the needle onto the Blue Danube. A waft of the most wonderful music, albeit scratchy, filled the little room.

Nothing would deter dancing at this point. Stan bowed graciously to the only girl, who seemed transformed to a virtual princess. He gallantly said, 'Would you . . . ?'

She raised her arms and was swept out the door into the spacious, empty garage on the arm of the handsome prince. Around and around they danced and the ballroom appeared, sumptuously decorated with cables, welding machines, flat tires and grease guns.

Dancing became infectious and we all began moving with the lilt. Stan saw the interest on our faces and stopped suddenly and stated, 'Dancing lessons will commence as of this minute. Jim, place your arms in this position in preparation for the great waltz.'

Phyllis took the lead with Jim while Stan chose another worker and with elbows high commenced at the downbeat. Apparently Jim had some music in his makeup for his dancing actually began to resemble the master's example. Listening and watching I was recalling my youth and the many waltzes in Northern Saskatchewan. But then we had not such a splendid ballroom and no expert leader or fine finesse.

Stan had each of us in turn dancing with Phyllis, all the while emphasising posture, timing and footwork. Finally our willing hostess more or less collapsed. We then crawled into our chariot and bumped off to camp, humming most of the way.

It seemed remarkable to experience such an instant transformation from the rough and busy camp life to that of the refined elegance of Europe. Although it was a simple event, the recollection of the lesson remained with us all for many a year. Now that Stan has passed on I consider it a cherished memory of my good friend.